Table of Contents

The Story So Far:

My name is Amphitrite, Goddess of the Sea, former consort to Poseidon, the King and God of the Sea. After my return to the surface world, and my trials in the Trench, I thought life would go smoothly. And then came the party the whole family was invited to. A party that none of us planned yet reeked of old power. A party from which none escaped unscathed.

1 – An Invitation from No One

The sea had been calm recently, which was odd because hurricane season had begun. Perhaps it was a sign of the peace I had found recently. Whatever the reason, I enjoyed it. I was going out for more swims, to check in with Rommel and the border guards, if not actually going into Atlantis herself. Something had felt off, and I hadn't been able to bring myself to go home properly. Regardless, I'd found myself going for longer and deeper swims than I had previously.

That day was one such day. The Pacific was calm, visibility was infinite, and I couldn't help but relish in the freedom the day brought. There was a sensation in my heart as if I was missing something important, but I couldn't place it. Rommel looked over at me as we coursed through the currents, and I watched my friend's face light up. We hadn't swum like this in an age, and I missed it. "My lad—" he began, but my side-eye cut him off. "Amph, you should probably head back. You know how Mathieu loses his mind when you have been gone for too long."

We had stopped swimming, and I sighed. "You're right, my friend, but this has been such a great day."

Rommel nodded as we made our way back to the surface. "I know, and we will have forever to swim the waves. Have no fear of that, my queen." We laughed, our heads breaking the surface as I lay out flat on the shimmering water.

"Same time next week?" I asked, looking over at Rommel. He nodded and smiled before diving deep and heading back to Atlantis. I closed my eyes, changed back to my *human* form, and teleported to my office at Nymphaeum. The sea-mist had barely dissipated around me when an invitation appeared on my desk. I picked it up carefully. The gold embossing was an elegant touch on the midnight blue background. But there was no sender information. While that had me intrigued, as did the idea of a party, it also threw up a couple of red flags.

I walked to my closet, pulling out a dress of light blue, airy feeling chiffon. I didn't bother with any other accouterments. Honestly, I wanted to be sure I could move if I needed to leave quickly. I sent a quick text to Mathieu to let him know I was heading to a party, then disappeared into the sea mist that encircled me whenever I teleported.

The scent of the ocean still wafting around me, I popped into the warehouse and looked around. "Who sent this invitation? I was barely back to the office when it arrived." My comment was a general one. If anyone answered, so be it.

Selene, Artemis, Athena, Eris, Eros, Clio, and even Zeus were already in attendance. Whatever the event was, it must have been big to pull the king out of his office. A few moments after I entered, Adrestia and Nike arrived. I also saw Thanatos, who had been hiding and trying to escape. Dikê showed up, looking as fierce as she had the last time I saw her, which was forever ago. Even Erebus, Atë, and Hekate made appearances, although the Primordial had conspicuously not arrived with the other two.

Most of the family were dressed to impress. We never missed an opportunity to show off. My heart skipped a beat when Poseidon walked in. He always looked amazing. But my heart soared when Dion arrived, and I resisted the urge to race into his arms. Instead, I took a drink from the only non-family member I could see in the room. He was good-looking in an unassuming way, but I didn't pay him much mind. The drink he was calling ambrosia had a sweet taste to it, and I found I desired another glass or two.

Dion and I made our way to each other, eventually. He had an extra glass of ambrosia, which he passed me, and I smiled gratefully. There was plenty of conversation throughout the room, so we didn't feel the need to speak to fill the void. Zeus gave a speech about parties and not getting together enough. He received cheers and applause, then the conversation turned to who had organized the party. Dion, while adamant he hadn't, wouldn't say no to taking credit. I had to chuckle. Although he could go elegant when necessary, the evening wasn't the normal shindig he'd have organized.

We didn't have much time to contemplate who brought us all together. Suddenly the lights lowered, and the sound of loud chanting came through hidden speakers. Voices overlapped as magic surged all around us. The black silk that decorated the walls wavered around the warehouse before falling. Glowing mirrors lined the interior. Runes were etched on each frame, along with the name of a god. They pulsed with power, all in sync with each other, but their focus was directed toward one individual god.

My eyes focused on one. I could feel the call of the sea in it, but not the calm seas I had emerged from earlier. The current was too strong for me to resist. I knew, for the briefest moment before I was dragged in, this was not a mirror with which to trifle. I tried reaching out for Dion, but my body wouldn't respond. Before I realized what was happening, I hit the floor and my mind careened into the mirror.

*****

"Trix, wake up. You go on in ten minutes!" a deep voice boomed through the PA system.

I was startled awake. The dream fading into the background. I shook my head as I looked into the mirror. Sleep matted my blonde hair. I would need to fix it quickly. I grabbed my large wire brush and ran it through my hair. Once I had the nice waves I preferred, I placed some decorative pins in to keep it out of my face.

My blue eyes sparkled as I touched up my mascara. The blurred, smoky look of my eye-shadow would be perfect for the set. I got up, found my red silk gown, a favourite of mine, and put it on. I tied the sash around my waist, pushing my breasts up, and smiled. "Bombshell, Trix. Perfect." A quick application of red lipstick, a kiss on the mirror, and I was out the door.

As I walked the hallways backstage, I looked out a window and saw that night had fallen over the New York skyline. I found myself backstage with just enough time to don a pair of strappy red heels before I heard Revan call my name. "And now, for the one you've all been waiting for, give it up for...Trix!" I burst onto the stage to a loud round of applause, my smile widening.

Some stars need drugs to get high. I needed the shine. I *loved* the spotlight. It made me feel amazing. That I was a talented singer only seemed to help. I was on the way to the top, something I had worked toward for years. Revan had told me earlier in the day that there would be agents from multiple record companies in the audience. That had just fueled the fire within me.

I could almost feel the tension in the crowd as the first notes of the song began. I shivered with anticipation. I opened my mouth, heard the crowd inhale with me, and began. Once I started, I couldn't stop. I *wouldn't* stop. I was addicted to the sensation.

My song choices for the night included some of my favourite covers that showcased my range and a few originals. Although I did not know where the titles had come from. *Siren Song*, *Maelstrom*, and *Wine Dark Sea* had come to me in a dream I'd had the previous night. I'd shaken it off when I was writing them and just plunged on. Anyway, it was going to be my night.

A face, well two faces, appeared before me as I was halfway through *Wine Dark Sea*, a song about the love of two stormy, powerful beings who were opposite yet complemented one another. One face had auburn hair and brown eyes, with a well-trimmed beard. The other had brown hair, blue eyes, and a clean-shaved face.

They seemed to call out to me, but their mouths let out no sounds. I tried to focus on the song, to shake the vision away, but the room spun around me. The last thing I knew, my head was cracking against the stage floor, and the crowd began screaming.

2 – A Star is Born

I woke slowly, the hum of the lights mixed almost painfully with the beeping of a machine nearby. I recognized it, a heart monitor, and I realized I must be in the hospital. I groaned deeply. This was not what I needed now, although…I paused as I felt a squeeze on my hand and looked down. Revan looked up at me, and I could tell that he'd spent the night here.

"Theresa, are you awake?" he asked, a soft voice among the machines in the room.

I stared at him, his eyes sagging from lack of sleep, and I smiled softly. "Yes, love, I'm fine." I sat up and watched the walls and ceiling melt into one another.

"Don't move. You've been out for almost a day. Apparently, you were highly salt deficient."

I squeezed my eyes shut and tried to stop the spinning around me, but with no luck. "What do you mean, salt deficient? I make sure, as do you, that my diet is well-balanced. I can't go around fainting on stage. What are…" I paused for a moment, unsure I wanted to hear the response. "What are people saying?"

"They loved it!" The excitement practically beamed off his face, and I couldn't help but smile. "People were so worried for you, and yet, the chanting going on, calling your name? 'Trixie, Trixie, Trixie!' It was exhilarating. I'm sorry you missed it. I've got two business cards from agents—"

"Who probably never want to hear my name again."

"Shush you. They want to hire you exclusively. I believe one of them called your voice *enrapturing* and *seraphic*." My jaw hit the floor.

"You're joking, even after the fainting?" Revan smiled, his face lighting up the room.

"I had one in my hand a few minutes before you went down, and the other came in about an hour ago." His hand squeezed mine, which was good because I felt my soul drifting away, and I needed grounding. "Let's get you home, Trix. You need to recover because I have some not-great news as well."

Revan's face darkened, and I could tell that whatever it was hurt him. "Revan, tell me what it is, please."

He just shook his head and got up, kissing my forehead. "I'll go get the doctor, wait here, and I'll be right back." With that, he walked out and left me worrying.

A few hours later, we were home, and I was curled up on the couch with a large bowl of chicken noodle soup. I had a warm blanket around me, and Revan was fidgeting. I could tell he was trying to phrase how to break the bad news to me, so I put the bowl on the side table to take his hands. "Just say it."

"Paul died yesterday."

I was glad that I had put the bowl down because I froze. "No, no, he didn't." I shook. Paul was my first friend, someone who took me under their wing and made me feel welcome when I moved to New York two decades ago. A total teddy bear. He couldn't be.

Revan just nodded. He knew we were close and that we'd drifted apart in the last couple of years because he didn't approve of me chasing fame. He wanted me to be true to myself and to my talent, not sell out. I pulled the blanket up around my face and broke down. Revan just moved forward and pulled me into his lap, letting me cry. I couldn't stop. My emotions spilled out, and I regretted every minute since I last saw him. I don't know how long we sat like that. The soup was cold; I knew that much.

When I had finally cried myself out, and Revan let me go, I moved back and picked up the soup. The first sip had me spitting it out. "There's no salt."

Revan looked at me carefully. "You don't normally put salt in your soup, Theresa." His voice was careful. I was still emotional, and he knew it. "Here, give me your bowl, and I'll add salt to it." He took the bowl and walked away as the visions that assaulted me on stage last night swam through my head again. So much was hitting me at once that a wave of nausea coursed through me. Revan returned with the soup as I hurled all over the floor.

The bowl dropped to the floor as Revan rushed over to me. "Trix! Are you ok?" I nodded and looked up at him.

"Ya, sorry. I don't know what's wrong with me." He lifted me back onto the couch and wrapped me up.

"I'll make you more soup. Just hold on." Revan hurried back into the kitchen and returned a few minutes later with another bowl of chicken noodle soup. I tasted it, and it still felt wrong. I scrunched my face up, and Revan chuckled. "Still wrong?"

"Ya, I'm not sure why, but I need more salt." Revan got up and brought me the saltshaker. I began shaking it into the bowl. Once I had seasoned it to my taste, Revan took a sip and coughed.

"Oh, dear lord." I just looked at him oddly. "It tastes like seawater in here. Seawater chicken broth. What's happened to you, Trix?"

I shook my head, confused. "What do you mean? It tastes normal to me." He just laughed, and I joined in. It felt good to laugh. For the moment, I forgot about Paul, the visions, and the fainting. I looked at my husband, my partner, my manager. He was trying to help, and I loved him immensely. But as I watched his face, long wavy brown hair, soft blue eyes, and a short, well-kept beard.

He looked so much like one of the men in my vision. I couldn't shake the fact that those men meant something to me, and yet, aside from the one that looked like Revan, I'd never seen them before. Certainly, the other one was foreign to me.

"Trix, I have an idea, but I'm not sure how keen you would be on it." His voice dropped an octave or so, and I looked up at him. "The agents want you to have another concert soon. I guess they want to hear you again without passing out." He snickered playfully and nudged me. "I thought maybe you could make it a benefit concert."

"A benefit concert?" I cocked my head at him.

"Yes, for Paul's family. You know the costs of funerals are expensive."

I smiled brightly at him. "That sounds like a perfect idea, Revan!" I beamed, pulled out my phone, and began planning the sets. Revan saw I was engulfed in the work and smiled, letting me work.

*****

A week passed, the evening of the concert arrived, and Revan introduced me to the two agents who wanted to sign me. I was nervous, but they gave me very generous offers. It would definitely be something to think about. Thunder rumbled outside, and I could almost feel the ocean rolling off the island. It wasn't something I'd ever noticed before, even having lived in New York for the last twenty years.

Revan went up on stage and did his usual bit, introducing me, and I breathed deeply. My salt intake this past week had skyrocketed to where doctors were baffled. I was too. I knew the quantity of salt I had put into my system this last week was unhealthy, even unsafe, but it just tasted normal.

I had found a midnight blue silk dress, one I hadn't worn in a long time, and slipped in on like it was a second skin. As he introduced me, I felt a wave roll through me. It was slightly disconcerting, but it passed quickly. I stepped up and beamed at the crowd, looking out over the sea of people. I took a deep breath and smiled softly.

"Thank you all for coming. I recently lost someone dear to me. Paul was a mentor, a friend, a colleague. He was a teacher, a confidante, a brother. His family is here, and I wish to honour him in the best way I know how. Paul was a musician, one of the best I ever knew, and I dedicate this entire show to him." The crowd was silent as I spoke and clapped politely. "All the proceeds will go to the family and to the charity work that was his life."

The crowd erupted in cheers, and I saw Paul's mother and brothers in the front row crying with happiness. I began my opening number and let the tears flow. The concert went well. I rode the high the crowd was giving me.

Once the show was over and I had said my farewell to Paul's family, Revan brought me to meet with the two agents again, and we got to talking about potential deals. I wasn't following the conversation closely, so I was glad for Revan. He knew what would be perfect for me, and by the end, I had a signed and sealed contract with one of the largest record companies on the eastern seaboard.

And yet, something was calling me, something I couldn't place but couldn't seem to fight.

3 – Bleed Through from the Sea

The concert was a success. We raised more than enough to cover Paul's funeral expenses, and I honoured my friend with music I knew he loved. On top of that, the record deal I had signed brought a new excitement as we began planning my future. Revan was right beside me the entire time, making sure that I was well taken care of. During one of the long and rather boring meetings, I drifted off to sleep. I hadn't been known to dream too deeply when I napped, but this one sucked me in. The call I'd been feeling recently found its way through.

*****

"Phee Phee, you look radiant today, my dear," the man beside me said. He was familiar to me, but even in the dream, I couldn't place his name.

"Thank you, and I must say, my love, that the sun on your skin is gorgeous," I licked my lips, "and you look damn tasty."

The man beside me laughed and wrapped his arms around me. "You know, we could always go for a swim. I do love how your skin glistens when it is wet." He leaned down to kiss me, and I felt my body melt effortlessly into his. The man lifted me easily off the sand and toward the water.

It was then I realized we were on a beach. I could tell by the smell it was the ocean and I recoiled, or at least I would have if I'd been awake. When the man walked into the surf, I could feel the strength of the sea flowing into me, consuming me, and I was confused. I was startled when we submerged ourselves.

*****

"No, I can't swim!" My voice rang through the boardroom as I woke up with a start. Revan had my hand in his, and I squeezed it for reassurance. I froze once I realized where I was and blushed furiously. "I am so sorry. I don't know what came over me."

The agent just chuckled. "Alright, so no cruises." I sighed in relief. Shortly thereafter, the meeting was adjourned, and Revan and I went home.

He was quiet the entire taxi ride back to our townhouse in SoHo, but I knew he had questions. I did too. This was just the latest in a string of odd behaviour for me. I opened the door to our place as Revan paid, and another wave hit me. But this was of loss, of grief. I placed my hands over my stomach and looked up as my husband came in behind me.

"Theresa?" He only called me by my full name when he was worried, so what he saw in my face must have shocked him. I looked in the foyer mirror and gasped. I was crying, and I had no idea why. "What is wrong?"

I shook my head as we curled up on the couch, his strong arms wrapping protectively around me. "I don't know. I feel like I've lost my world. And yet, you're right here." Revan kissed my head gently, and I breathed him in, falling into his scent. "Why did we never have children?" I muttered softly.

"I..." His face fell. "Did you forget, Trix? Did you forget Melissa?" At the sound of her name, I gasped, and the memory flashed before my eyes again. Ten years ago, a hospital room, joy hanging in the air, and then no crying. The pain of childbirth numbed instantly when I realized that my daughter had been stillborn.

"Oh gods, why would I forget that?!" I sobbed harshly. "Why is this happening? Why, when our lives are finally coming together, am I crashing around you?" I couldn't keep the despair out of my voice. "These dreams, this salt thing... All of it. Why now?"

"Could it be cold feet? You're not really sure you want to do this?" He asked kindly as his hands rested over mine against my abdomen.

"No, I've wanted this since I was a child. And you, I want you more than life itself. I just feel so *connected* to these two men who appear in my visions and dreams. Like the bond that I have with them is soul-deep. I can't explain it."

"What dream?" Revan asked, and I realized that I hadn't explained the one from this afternoon. I recapped what happened, and Revan's arms wrapped tighter around me. "Well, I can't say I care for this new thread pulling you away from me." His voice was dark, and I barely caught the hint of threat in it. "Any names to go along with these faces?"

"No," I shook my head, "I wish I had something to go on, something more tangible than a face." I closed my eyes for a moment. "He called me, or the me in the dream, *Phee Phee*, which is absurd. It sounds made up. It sounds weird." Revan rested his head on mine, and I felt him breathe behind me. "Never mind these dumbass fantasies. What was discussed that I missed?"

I felt my husband smile and kiss my neck. "First concert will be an outdoor gig at Central Park this weekend. It's a good thing you have been performing all along, so your repertoire will be solid."

I looked up at him and smiled, kissing him gently. "As long as I have you by my side, nothing will go wrong." And yet, inside, I was churning. It seemed these visions came while I was on stage, while I was the centre of attention. It was only brief flashes the rest of the time.

"And I have no plans to go anywhere." Revan leaned into the kiss, and I felt the passion build within. I rolled around in his arms and smiled up at him. It had been a while because Revan hadn't wanted to while I was feeling off, but I needed this. I needed him. His own fire met mine, and we melted into each other. I barely noticed that it had begun raining outside, but it was always raining in New York.

The evening passed in pleasure. When we woke the following morning, the rain had ebbed off, and I decided to head out for a walk. Revan was still asleep on the pile of pillows and blankets on our living room floor, so I slipped out quietly to not disturb him.

The city was still damp after the summer rain, and I wandered the streets, both major and side streets, letting my feet guide me. I meandered through SoHo until I reached the west side of Manhattan, and I was looking out over the Hudson River. I had spent my entire life afraid of the ocean, of the sea, pretty much of all large bodies of water.

Yet, I was tempted to throw myself off and see what would happen. But why, though? Why was I thinking that? Why did I forget my beautiful Melissa? I wanted to scream but also knew I couldn't. It was too early. Perhaps I would come back at night and let it all out. The things I couldn't tell Revan, like how much he resembled the one and how much pain came when I thought of him. Or how much love I felt when I imagined the auburn-haired man.

I found a bench nearby and sat down, letting the air waft over me. We were a distance from the ocean, but I could almost feel the Atlantic calling to me. It was both confusing and warming. Like a lover I had never known, beckoning me home. *Home…* The flash of a glowing city under the sea shone before my eyes, so clear I reached out to grab it. I had to figure out what was causing this, why I was so torn between reality and my dreams.

My phone rang suddenly, and I saw Revan's face light up when I answered the Facetime call. "Trix, where are you?" he asked quickly after my hello.

"I'm in a little park on the Hudson." His mouth fell open. I had never come to the shorelines before, so why now? "What's up, love?"

"Oh, other than the concert in two days?" I nodded with a smile. "You got your first advance from the agency." This time my mouth hung open. "Come home and get dressed. We're going out for the night. Dinner, a show, the works!"

"I'm on my way, Revan. What did you have in mind?" I got up and began the walk back home.

Revan grinned widely. "I know you've wanted to try Per Se, so I called and got a reservation." With that, I broke into a run. I'd been wanting to eat there since it opened, but getting a reservation was nearly impossible unless you were *someone*. I guess I was now.

It took me longer to get home than it did to get to the water because I had to think about my travel. When I burst through the door panting, Revan simply laughed at me and guided me up to the shower. "I've picked out the perfect dress. Go get ready, and we'll make an evening of it."

I kissed his cheek and raced up the stairs to the master bathroom. I jumped into the shower, and the heat on my skin felt amazing after the run and cool morning air. Once the water ran cool, I stepped out and made my way into the bedroom. The dress that Revan had picked out was a gorgeous grey-blue satin evening gown that I knew would set off my blonde curls and blue eyes. It was Revan's favourite dress, and I just smiled. He had done so much to get me here. I owed him everything.

Tonight would be perfect. I would not have any visions
or drift off. It would just be him and me. Nothing was
going to mess with what I had, and what I had coming.

4 – The Waking Dream

The day of the concert arrived. It was to be my debut with the recording label. My agent was a man named Gerald, who seemed vaguely familiar, though I couldn't place from where. He smiled at me and spoke pleasantly enough, but I could tell there was a strength to him that belied his gentle exterior.

He guided me to the side of the stage a few minutes before I was to go on, and smiled down at me. "Alright, Am— Trix, you got this. There are over a thousand people in the crowd, so just go out on stage and shine like the star you are."

I looked at him as he stumbled on my name, but he shrugged it off. "A thousand?" I had never sung in front of that many people before, and I could feel the exhilaration building. It was almost orgasmic.

"More, if we can bribe the fire department," he replied with a chuckle. "Now, Revan will announce you like normal, but just go out there and kill it." He squeezed my shoulders gently and disappeared backstage.

I took a few deep breaths and centered myself. I could feel the crowd from here, undulating with excitement, and the high began. Once I heard my name called, and I burst onto stage, I knew that Theresa Gill would be no more. I would only be Trix. This was everything I had wanted for my entire life, and nothing was going to take it away from me.

I felt my name called, the introduction beginning, and made my way out onto the stage. The lights shone down on me, the crowd roared, and I was in Heaven. If I died this very instant, I would be happy.

"Rock their world, love," Revan whispered as he kissed me before departing the stage. I smiled back and then looked out over the sea of people. I could feel their desires, their needs, their wants, as if I were in tune with each and every individual, and it was addictive.

"Welcome and thank you for coming!" I gave a small curtsy and beamed out over the crowd. "My name is Trix Gill, and this is *Wine Dark Sea*!" I began the song, luring them all into my voice, and lost myself in the music. No faces, no visions disturbed me this time, and when it came time for the intermission, I was on such a high from everything, I didn't know which way was up. I stumbled down the stairs once I was out of sight of the crowd, and Revan caught me.

"Whoa! Are you alright, Trix?" I nodded dumbly and smiled. "Do you want to meet some of your adoring fans?"

"Absolutely!" I was elated. I loved meeting my fans, getting to know them, and how my music touched them. "Let's go!" I was off, a bullet out of Revan's arms, and he laughed, trying to rein me in. As Revan guided me to the crowd, I felt the presence of someone behind me, but when I looked, no one was there. I shrugged it off and began talking with my fans, some of whom had been following me since my very first set almost a decade and a half ago, and I chatted with them the most.

Near the end of the intermission, a man caught my eye, warm in face, with soft brown eyes and auburn hair, and a name escaped my lips at barely a whisper, "Dionysos." Revan caught the sound and looked at me before I took off in a run, chasing after him. I barely heard my husband in the distance racing after me.

The figure left Central Park, heading east towards the river. I didn't know why I was following him. I didn't know the man, and yet my heart told me I did. When we got to the water's edge, the vision floated neatly out over the water, and I just stared at him. "Who are you!?" I called out, my voice ragged from the running.

"Who are you talking to?" Revan's voice sounded from behind me. I spun around, not realizing he was there, and froze. My husband, the man I loved, had a pistol pointed at me. "Trix, you're not going to destroy my future by leaving me!"

"No!" I took a step forward, and his hand shook, causing me to stop. "I'm not leaving, but I need to know what this is all about and why it affects me when I'm singing."

"We'll ask Gerald. He'll know. He knows everything. Now, come back to the concert and finish the set." I shook my head, surprising us both. "No? No! You've never denied me anything, *anything* I've asked for, and yet you deny me this?!"

"I can't go back right now Revan, if I do, I'll ruin the show. I know I will. I'll pass out, or worse. I can feel something dark hanging over me. I have to..." I turned back to the river, watching the waves lap against the jetty. "I need to jump in," I muttered.

"If you do, you're as good as dead. But hey, maybe I can sell that and boost my own career." I spun back around to him.

"Is that all you care about, your own career? Not the fact that I'm going mad here?" Revan just laughed, cold and harsh, nothing I had ever heard from him before.

"All I wanted was you and fame...and Melissa." I shuddered and wrapped my arms around myself. "You killed our baby somehow. Your body decided to kill it, and for that," Revan closed his eyes and fired without warning, the bullet piercing my stomach, "you need to feel this pain."

I screamed out, clutching my abdomen as I fell backward into the river. Instead of calling out for my husband or for my unborn daughter, the only name I could hear, the only one that came to me, was the one I uttered earlier. "Dion!"

*****

I awoke in the warehouse, sitting up suddenly, not sure of where I was. I looked around me, seeing the faces and people who were familiar and not. It was like when you wake from a dream and can't remember that you're no longer dreaming. My eyes fell onto Dionysos

and then Poseidon, and I realized those were the two faces the dream me had seen, the ones who were connecting her to this reality. I scrambled up and looked down at myself and the mirror that had my name on it. It was shattered, and a faint mist of glass hung in the air. I didn't know if I was the first to wake, but I couldn't stay. My hands went to my stomach, and I ran for a bucket, retching into it before I disappeared, taking the garbage with me.
Something was wrong. Something was terribly wrong.

Author Bio

Natalie Bartley is a Canadian Adult-Fantasy author. Natalie has been writing for most of her teenage and adult life but started publishing those stories in December 2019 with her first book, *Love and Pain in Zion*. Natalie's faith as a polytheistic witch leads her to many storylines involving the gods which surround her. She lives with her partner and stepson in Bowmanville, Ontario and is also completing her clergy status with the Correllian Nativist Tradition. They hope to one day open their own Pagan store together.

The last chapter of *Maelstrom*, Nisos, and part of Beached, were written in collaboration with Peter Farmer, the scribe for Dionysos. I use our words with his permission. Thank you, Peter, for being an excellent writing partner.

For more of Amphitrite's story, check out:
https://www.inthepantheon.com/author/amphitrite/

Thank you to Brandon Fero for doing the cover work, it is gorgeous!!! Go take a look at his work @BranconFero on Twitter!

Other Titles by Natalie Bartley

Love and Pain in Zion

Gods at the End of the World:
The Iridescent Kitchen Sylph

Apotheosis

The Lady of the Sea:
Maelstrom
A Week in Korinth
Forgotten Gods: Amphitrite